Dear Parents and Educators,

Welcome to Penguin Young Readers! As parents and educators, you
know that each child develops at his or her own pace—in terms of
speech, critical thinking, and, of course, reading. Penguin Young
Readers recognizes this fact. As a result, each Penguin Young Readers
book is assigned a traditional easy-to-read level (1–4) as well as a
Guided Reading Level (A–P). Both of these systems will help you choose
the right book for your child. Please refer to the back of each book
for specific leveling information. Penguin Young Readers features
esteemed authors and illustrators, stories about favorite characters,
fascinating nonfiction, and more!

Miss Bindergarten and the Secret Bag

LEVEL **2**

GUIDED
READING
LEVEL **E**

This book is perfect for a **Progressing Reader** who:
- can figure out unknown words by using picture and context clues;
- can recognize beginning, middle, and ending sounds;
- can make and confirm predictions about what will happen in the text; and
- can distinguish between fiction and nonfiction.

Here are some **activities** you can do during and after reading this book:
- Compare/Contrast: Both Alex and Miss Bindergarten have surprises
  to share with the class. How are their surprises alike? How are they
  different?
- Make Connections: Pretend that you are the Star of the Week. What
  would you bring in your secret bag? Work with the child to draw a picture
  of their "surprise" and write a few sentences to describe it.

Remember, sharing the love of reading with a child is the best gift
you can give!

—Bonnie Bader, EdM
  Penguin Young Readers program

*Penguin Young Readers are leveled by independent reviewers applying the standards developed by Irene Fountas
and Gay Su Pinnell in *Matching Books to Readers: Using Leveled Books in Guided Reading*, Heinemann, 1999.

For Parker Joseph, just two —JS

For Lucia, Miss Bindergarten's
new Fairy Godmother. Thank you —AW

Penguin Young Readers
Published by the Penguin Group
Penguin Group (USA) Inc., 375 Hudson Street, New York, New York 10014, USA
Penguin Group (Canada), 90 Eglinton Avenue East, Suite 700, Toronto, Ontario M4P 2Y3, Canada
(a division of Pearson Penguin Canada Inc.)
Penguin Books Ltd, 80 Strand, London WC2R 0RL, England
Penguin Ireland, 25 St Stephen's Green, Dublin 2, Ireland (a division of Penguin Books Ltd)
Penguin Group (Australia), 707 Collins Street, Melbourne, Victoria 3008, Australia
(a division of Pearson Australia Group Pty Ltd)
Penguin Books India Pvt Ltd, 11 Community Centre, Panchsheel Park, New Delhi—110 017, India
Penguin Group (NZ), 67 Apollo Drive, Rosedale, Auckland 0632, New Zealand
(a division of Pearson New Zealand Ltd)
Penguin Books (South Africa), Rosebank Office Park, 181 Jan Smuts Avenue,
Parktown North 2193, South Africa
Penguin China, B7 Jiaming Center, 27 East Third Ring Road North,
Chaoyang District, Beijing 100020, China

Penguin Books Ltd, Registered Offices: 80 Strand, London WC2R 0RL, England

Text copyright © 2013 by Joseph Slate. Illustrations copyright © 2013 by Ashley Wolff. All rights reserved.
Published by Penguin Young Readers, an imprint of Penguin Group (USA) Inc., 345 Hudson Street,
New York, New York 10014. Manufactured in China.

Library of Congress Cataloging-in-Publication Data is available.

ISBN 978-0-448-46803-7 (pbk)   10 9 8 7 6 5 4 3 2 1
ISBN 978-0-8037-3988-8 (hc)   10 9 8 7 6 5 4 3 2 1

Miss Bindergarten
and the Secret Bag

by Joseph Slate
illustrated by Ashley Wolff

Penguin Young Readers
An Imprint of Penguin Group (USA) Inc.

Meet Miss Bindergarten.

Here is her class.

They call her Miss B.

Today Brenda sees a new chair.

6

"May I sit on it?" says Brenda.

"No," says Miss B.

"It is for the Star."

"Who is the Star?" says Adam.

"His name starts with **A**," says Miss B.

"My name starts with **A**!"

says Adam.

"Yes," says Miss B.

"You are the Star.

Now you may shine."

The next day Adam brings a bag.

"It is my secret bag," says Adam.

"What is in your bag?"

says Brenda.

"Here is a hint," says Adam.

"It is red."

"Is it a red ball?" says Franny.

"Is it a red car?" says Danny.

"Is it a red fire truck?"

says Brenda.

"Yes!" says Adam.

"I love fire trucks!"

The next day Adam sees

a BIG new chair.

"Today I have a secret,"

says Miss B.

"Think of the fire truck."

Rap!
Rap!

Someone is at

the door.

"Oh, oh," says Adam.

"Is it Chief Dave?"

"Hello, Chief Dave," says Miss B.

"Please sit down."

"I have a secret, too,"

says Chief Dave.

"Shut your eyes, Adam."

"A red hat!" says Adam.

"Thank you, Chief Dave!"

"I love red."